APR - - 2015

Green River

By WonKyeong Lee

Illustrated by HyeWon Yang

Language Arts Consultant: Joy Cowley

NORWOODHOUSE PRESS

Chicago, Illinois

DEAR CAREGIVER MySELF ▮ ▮▮ Bookshelf is a series of books that support children's social emotional learning. SEL has been proven to promote not only the development of self-awareness, responsibility, and positive relationships, but also academic achievement.

Current research reveals that the part of the brain that manages emotion is directly connected to the part of the brain that is used in cognitive tasks, such as: problem solving, logic, reasoning, and critical thinking—all of which are at the heart of learning.

SEL is also directly linked to what are referred to as 21st Century Skills: collaboration, communication, creativity, and critical thinking. MySELF Bookshelf offers an early start that will help children build the competencies for success in school and life.

In these delightful books, young children practice early reading skills while learning how to manage their own feelings and how to be considerate of other perspectives. Each book focuses on aspects of SEL that help children develop social competence that will benefit them in their relationships with others as well as in their school success. The charming characters in the stories model positive traits such as: responsibility, goal setting, determination, patience, and celebrating differences. At the end of each story, you will find a letter that highlights the positive traits and an activity or discussion to help your child apply SEL to his or her own life.

Above all, the most important part of the reading experience is to have fun and enjoy it!

Sincerely,

Shannon Cannon

Shannon Cannon, Ph.D.
Literacy and SEL Consultant

Norwood House Press • P.O. Box 316598 • Chicago, Illinois 60631
For more information about Norwood House Press please visit our website at www.norwoodhousepress.com or call 866-565-2900.

Shannon Cannon – Literacy and SEL Consultant
Joy Cowley – English Language Arts Consultant
Mary Lindeen – Consulting Editor

Library of Congress Cataloging-in-Publication Data
    Lee, WonKyeong.
   Green River / by WonKyeong Lee ; illustrated by HyeWon Yang.
     pages cm. -- (MySelf bookshelf)
   Summary: "When the little beaver Kobe discovers that his home at Green River has become polluted with trash and is no longer safe, Kobe decides to take action. With the help of his friends, they remove the trash from the river and work together to build an amazing playground"-- Provided by publisher.
   ISBN 978-1-59953-660-6 (library edition : alk. paper) -- ISBN 978-1-60357-720-5 (ebook)
   [1. Rivers--Fiction. 2. Beavers--Fiction. 3. Water--Pollution--Fiction. 4. Environmental protection--Fiction.] I. Yang, HyeWon, illustrator. II. Title.
   PZ7.1.L44Gr 2015
   [E]--dc23
               2014030337

Manufactured in the United States of America in Stevens Point, Wisconsin.
263N—122014

Green River was where the beavers lived.
Little Beaver Kobe loved Green River.
Along its banks were trees
that were good for beaver houses,
and in the water there were many fish.

4

6

But it wasn't only the beavers
who liked Green River.
People came in their cars.
They had picnics, went swimming
and caught fish.

8

Before long, the river was full of trash
thrown away by the people.
The beavers swam beside broken glass.
They caught their tails in bits of plastic.

9

The beavers held a meeting
about the polluted river.

"Let's move away from here," they said.
"Let's go and find another home."

But Kobe had a different idea.
"No! Green River is our home.
Why don't we clean up the trash?"

But no one listened to Kobe.

The next day, Kobe got up early
and started to carry the trash away
from his Green River home.
He worked all morning.
He worked all afternoon.
He was even working at night.

14

The other beavers laughed.

"Look at Kobe! He is so dirty!"

"He smells terrible!"

"Kobe is very strange!"

Kobe did not notice.

He went on cleaning the river.

16

The adult beavers were ready
to move to another river
when they noticed something had changed.
"Look! Green River is cleaner.
There isn't so much trash."

Kobe's friends also noticed
that the river was cleaner.
"Kobe takes the trash away.
Let's follow him to see
what he does with it."

18

Plod, plod, plod.
Kobe carried a big bundle of trash on his back.
He went into the woods.

In the middle of the woods
was a huge heap of trash
that Kobe had collected.
He had cleaned and dried it
so that it did not smell.

"Kobe! What are you doing?"
asked his friends.

Kobe looked at them.
"If I pick up the trash,
I can save Green River,
and I can do something else
that is just as wonderful."

"Can we help you?"
his friends asked.

Kobe told his friends about his plan
and they helped him gather trash
from the river.
Plod, plod, plod.

The adult beavers noticed
the line of little beavers.
"What are they doing?"
asked the adult beavers,
and they followed the little beavers.

25

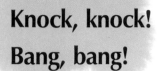

Knock, knock!
Bang, bang!
The little beavers were
using the trash to make
an amazing playground.

"This is a tire swing."

"This is a slippery slide."

"These are climbing bars."

"These are musical instruments."

25

When the adult beavers saw the fine playground,
they were ashamed.

Kobe and the children had worked hard
to make the river beautiful again.
The adults changed their minds.
They would not leave Green River.
"Thank you, Kobe. Thank you, children."

Today, Green River is the only river in the world that
has a wonderful playground for young beavers.

Dear Kobe,

Thank you so much for all of the hard work you did when you cleaned up Green River. The rest of us were ready to move away, but you were a very careful and creative thinker. You thought of a better way to solve our problem.

We didn't know what you were doing at first. We are sorry that we laughed at you and made fun of you. Thank goodness you just kept on working so hard. You showed us that we didn't have to leave our home after all—we could clean it up and stay in Green River instead.

We didn't know what you were doing with all of that trash either, but then we realized that you had not just one very good idea but two! We would have never guessed that we could have reused the trash to turn it into such a wonderful playground. It takes a lot of creative thinking to come up with an idea like that. We are so glad that you shared your good ideas with us!

Your friends and neighbors,
The Beavers of Green River

SOCIAL AND EMOTIONAL LEARNING FOCUS

Caring for the Environment

There is a saying, "One man's trash is another man's treasure." The little beavers learned this. By removing the trash, they cleaned up the river. But that wasn't all! They made it useful again. Some people call this upcycling—which is the process of making trash or useless materials into new and better things.

You can upcycle! Here is an idea to get you started. You can make fun games out of things that might get thrown away.

Plastic Bottle Bowling

- Save 10 plastic bottles (for example, 16 oz. water, juice, or soda bottles)

- Arrange them like bowling pins (they should not touch)

- Use a tennis ball to knock them over

- You can number the lids to score points. The most difficult pins to knock down should have higher points.

You can think of your own ideas to make games or crafts from items that might be headed to the trash!

Reader's Theater

Reader's Theater is an interactive approach to reading that allows students to understand each story through dramatic interpretation. By involving students in reading, listening, and speaking activities, they provide an integrated approach for students to develop fluency and comprehension. A Reader's Theater edition of this book is available online. You can access the script by scanning the QR code to the right or visit our website at:
http://www.norwoodhousepress.com/greenriver.aspx